Aliens in Underpants Save the World

To Ben, my pants-tastic illustrator ~ C. F.

For Matilda, with love ~ B. C.

ISBN 978-0-545-44739-3

Text copyright © 2009 by Claire Freedman.
Illustrations copyright © 2009 by Ben Cort.
All rights reserved. Published by Scholastic Inc., 557 Broadway, New York, NY 10012,
by arrangement with Aladdin, an imprint of Simon & Schuster Children's Publishing Division.
SCHOLASTIC and associated logos are trademarks and/or registered trademarks of Scholastic Inc.

12 11 10 9 8 7 6 5 4   12 13 14 15 16 17/0

Printed in the U.S.A.   08

This edition first printing, February 2012

The text of this book was set in Plumbsky Black.

Aliens in Underpants Save the World

ILLUSTRATED BY
Ben Cort

CLAIRE FREEDMAN

SCHOLASTIC INC.
New York Toronto London Auckland
Sydney Mexico City New Delhi Hong Kong

Aliens love underpants.

It's lucky that they do.

For underpants saved our universe.

Sounds crazy, but it's true!

On one pants-pinching mission,
   the aliens zoomed through space.
The spaceships shook and wobbled.
Their hearts began to race.

Their radars bleeped, their sirens wailed,
    on came the warning light!
Heading straight for planet Earth
    was one huge meteorite!

Meanwhile, on Earth, the scientists
had such an awful fright.
"What's THAT?" they gulped
in horror,
"Picked up on our satellite?"

The fire engines came racing,
   police and air rescue, too,
But with just four hours till impact,
   there was little they could do!

Down to Earth the aliens shot,
and they jumped out with
a shout,
"No time to lose, if Earth blows up,
our underpants supply runs out!"

They took undies down from clotheslines,
  and raided all the stores.
They sneaked inside our houses
  and pulled bloomers out of
  drawers.

The aliens stitched the underwear,
and proudly they unfurled,
The most GINORMOUS pair of
underpants made in the whole
wide world!

Quickly with their spaceships,
    they stretched the underpants in place.
And when the meteor landed,
    it zoomed back to outer space!

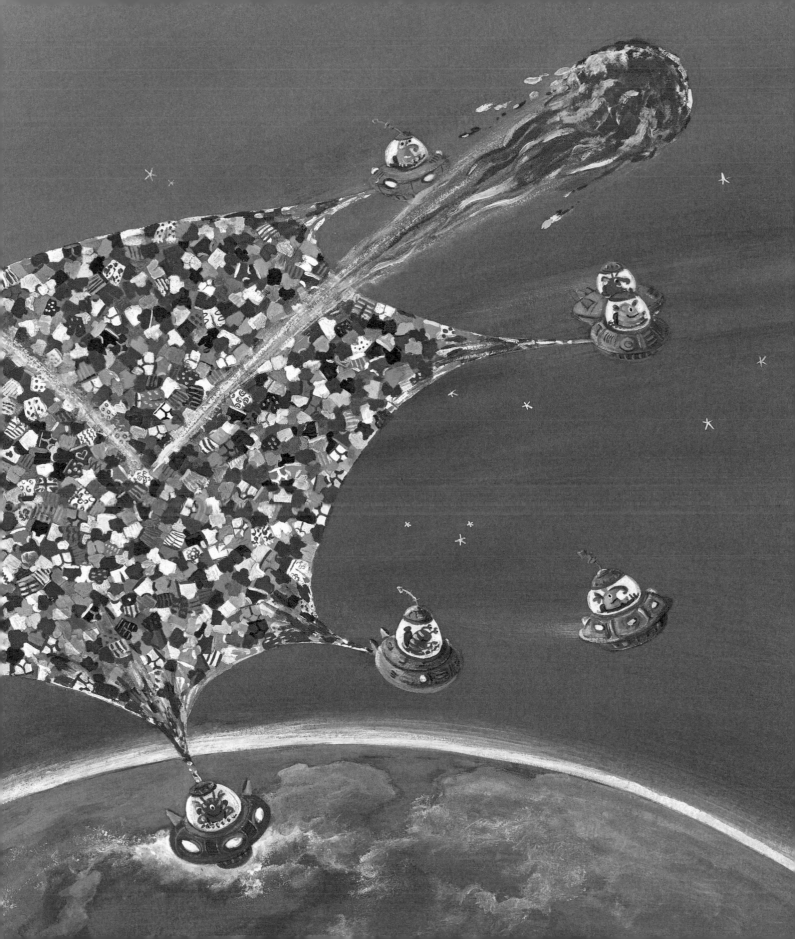

"The meteorite has vanished!"
gasped the people in surprise,
"We thought we saw huge underpants,
but can't believe our eyes!"

Back at home the aliens cheered,
"Our pants plan was fantastic!
We saved the Earth with underpants
   so stretchy and elastic!"

So should your pants go missing,
there's no need to make a fuss.
Let the aliens have their fun.
They've done SO much for us!